Written by
Phil
Roxbee Cox

S0-AGP-696

Photographed
by
Sue Atkinson

Designed by
Becky
Halverson

Project
Co-ordinator:
Rupert Heath

IMPORTANT MESSAGE TO THE READER

Who stole the Black Diamond?

That's the question on everyone's lips and you, dear reader, have just been hired to find the answer. By the time you've reached page 41 you should be able to tell whodunnit. There are clues lurking throughout the book, but there are plenty of false clues too. All is not always what it seems.

As you work your way through the story, you'll find questions that need answering. They are there to make sure that you're keeping your eyes peeled and are using your detecting skills. To solve this case, however, you'll need to make your own deductions and to use your best powers of reasoning.

Here's a list of possible suspects. Check them out. Then you should be able to say who it was who stole the Black Diamond. Good luck

P.S. If you're stuck, you'll find some helpful hints on page 42. The answers are on pages 43 to 47. You'll find the solution to the whole mystery on page 48.

POSSIBLE SUSPECTS

Gideon T. Thackery III – curator of the Earl E. Byrdd Institute

Gertrude Rook – lawyer

Christen Hans Anderfeet – diamond expert

Percy Smart – bank manager

Sid Nasty – crazy criminal mastermind

Dr. Robin Swyne-Thevin – scientist

Spikey Muffin – jewel thief

Herbert 'Swifty' Morris – courier

Ed Meanstreets – Private Investigator

PLUS all members of SNATCH, and anyone else you might run into.

Series Editor:
Gaby Waters

READ ALL ABOUT IT

Time: Thursday, 8:47pm
Place: Brenda's Breakfast Bar

Your orange juice may be murky, but your mission is clear. The *Black Diamond* has been stolen and you've been hired to find it. The newspaper clippings should give you some useful information. The iced doughnut should give you some energy.

How much is the Black Diamond worth?
Where was the missing safe found?

FR...

Free Dog Shampoo
Voucher: 001397B

Count Lukki's will 'is missing'

from our legal correspondent

Both copies of the will of billionaire Count Uself Lukki have disappeared according to his lawyer of sixty years, Ms. Gertrude Sparrow. She told reporters "Lukki recently drew up a new will, keeping a copy for himself and giving me one to put in my safe. Unfortunately, his copy cannot be found and neither can my safe."

The lawyer went on to ex... that she was not allowed... what was in the missi... will. "All will be re... will has been rec...

'Mr Diamond' dies peacefully at home

Dan Eagleberg

Count Uself Lukki, the internationally-famous philanthropist, philatelist, and collector of some of the world's most precious of precious gems has died in his sleep at home. He would have been 120 years old next Tuesday.

The late Count acquired his nickname 'Mister Diamond', his wealth and his many different collections by discovering the Lukki Diamond back in 1952. He went on to become one of the world's greatest collectors of everything from diamonds to silk vegetables. It is believed that he has left all of these collections to the Earl E. Byrdd Institute.

Though extremely rich, the Count was in the habit of giving his friends the same gift every year: a sparkling glass paperweight. He had homes in New York and in the capital city of Verstroodl in the Republic of Olanga.

Count Lukki as a baby

...out ...f the ...been ...uld be ...picking ...st night ...riends.

being co... One line of investigation is that the *Black Diamond* might have been stolen by the gang of international jewel thieves SNATCH. They are believed to be behind a number of attempted break-ins at the world-famous *Black Eagle Diamond Mine*.

...ke eater o...

Who stole the Black Diamond?
Police baffled

...eems to know what it ...ut everyone knows

Lukki's p... of missing...

from our own correspo...

Police investigating the disa... the safe containing the late Co... will now suspect that it was stole... villain, Archie Rook. Mr. Rook us... the Count's plumber and was me... leak in the office of the Count's la... ...time of the disappearance of...

2

Sparrow marries Rook

Thurs: Ms. Gertrude Sparrow, lawyer to the la[te] Count Uself L[ukki] yesterday annou[nced] married conv[...] Archie Roo[k]... Mr. Rook, [...] accused of s[...] containing [...] Lukki will. Mr. Rook and the [...] Miss Sparrow were [married] at a civil ceremony. "[...] have been a naughty [...] [b]ut he's a great plumber [...] love him," the newlywe[d] [M]rs. Rook told waitin[g] [re]porters.

'Safe and well'

Tues: Well-known pe[...] crook and plumber Archi[e] Rook is being questioned [by] police regarding the s[...] missing from the offices [of] Miss Gertrude Sparrow. Miss Sparrow's missing safe was found under [...] Rook's bed when [...] local detectives [...] searched his apartment last night.

Missing 'Lukki will' found

Dan Eagleberg

A copy of the missing will of the late Count Uself Lukki was found yesterday by his lawyer for almost sixty years, Ms. Gertrude Sparrow. "Silly me! The will was in my handbag all the time." she said. "It was never even in the safe. As was widely reported, Lukki has left his collections to the Earl E. Byrdd Institute.

Black Diamond missing

The $2½ milli[on] Black Diamo[nd] mentioned [in] Count L[ukki's] will, is s[...] to hav[e] [...] given [...] E. [...] I[nstitute]

Mrs Gertrude Rook (formerly Ms. Sparrow) at a press conference.

Stop Press

Police suspect the SNATCH gang could be behind missing Black Diamond. Sid [...]sty seen near Earl [E.] [B]yrdd Institute.

Black Diamond missing

[t]he most valuable item listed in Count Lukki's will and left to the Earl E. Byrdd Institute is missing. "We can't find it anywhere," says lawyer Gertrude Sparrow. "The Count's instructions were clear. He said to arrange to have Thackery send the Black Diamond along with the original packaging with which he, the Count, first received it from Olanga. The count added that Thackery was an expert and that he would realize the Black Diamond's value and would place it on display at the Institute.'"

Gideon T. Thackery III told reporters "I was amazed to find the package empty, apart from some tissue paper. The Black Diamond has been stolen!" All other collections left to the Institute

philanthropist n. a person who performs charitable acts [from Greek *philos* meaning loving and *anthropos* meaning man]

philatelist n. a collector and studier of postage stamps [from the French *philatélie*]

TODAY'S BREAKFAST SPECIAL

Orange Juice

*

Grapefruit

*

Cereal

*

Pancakes

*

Toast

*

Coffee

*

Stomachache

3

Nzib Irxph

Ofppr

Drohlm

Szilow Hnrgs

4

A COLLECTION OF CLUES

Time: Monday, 12:24pm
Place: Office of Bequests & Acquisitions,
   Earl E. Byrdd Institute

The first name on your list of possible suspects is the assistant deputy curator, Gideon T. Thackery III. He's busy right now, so you snoop around this room where they store some of the new collections. Each collection has been coded with the donor's name. No gems here, but there is one of Lukki's other collections.

Which collection was donated by Count Lukki?
Who donated the other items?

Ixias pyrene insignis

Ravadeba aglea

Byasa polyeucte termessus

Catopsilia crocale

Qrn Xzigvi

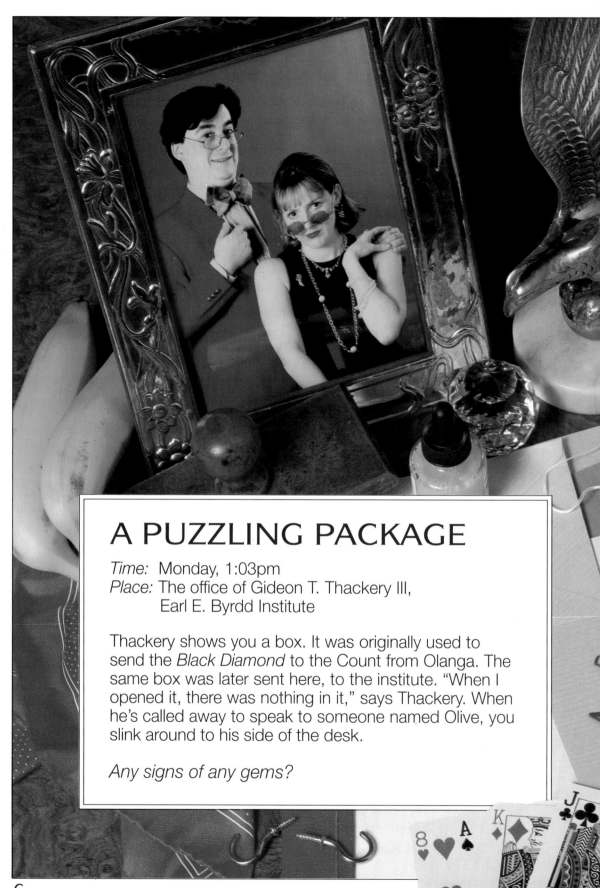

A PUZZLING PACKAGE

Time: Monday, 1:03pm
Place: The office of Gideon T. Thackery III,
Earl E. Byrdd Institute

Thackery shows you a box. It was originally used to send the *Black Diamond* to the Count from Olanga. The same box was later sent here, to the institute. "When I opened it, there was nothing in it," says Thackery. When he's called away to speak to someone named Olive, you slink around to his side of the desk.

Any signs of any gems?

Count U. Lukki,
Lukki Tower,
Billionaire Drive,
N.Y., N.Y.

A MYSTERIOUS GIFT

Time: Monday, 3:10pm
Place: The Sidewalk Cafe,
         outside New Central Station

Next on the list is Gertrude Rook. You stop for a bite to eat, before catching a train to her office. You squeeze your cake and milkshake onto the corner of a table. It's occupied by a woman hiding behind a newspaper. You're about to sit down, when she pushes a present out from under her paper. "For you," she says "Follow the advice on it. A detective is on our trail."

What does the advice say?

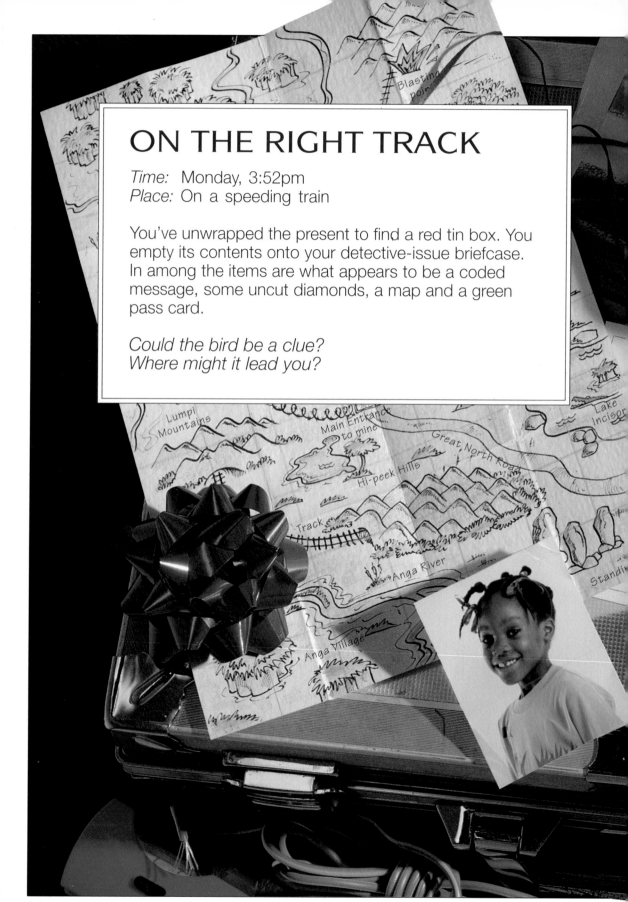

ON THE RIGHT TRACK

Time: Monday, 3:52pm
Place: On a speeding train

You've unwrapped the present to find a red tin box. You empty its contents onto your detective-issue briefcase. In among the items are what appears to be a coded message, some uncut diamonds, a map and a green pass card.

Could the bird be a clue?
Where might it lead you?

MLRRV JOBURF

OXUJOWXYZVU,

AOL RLF VWLUZ

AOL ZPAL

VMMPJL AV

AOL I.L.K.T.

DOHA FVB ULLK

PZ PU AOLYL

ZUHAJO

DUSTY SECRETS

Time: Monday, 5:15pm
Place: Offices of Mrs. Gertrude Rook, Lawyer

According to the newspapers, Mrs Rook was Miss Sparrow before she married the man who stole her safe. The door to her office is unlocked, but there's no one here. In fact, it looks like there hasn't been anyone here in ages ... and there's not much of interest.

Or is there?

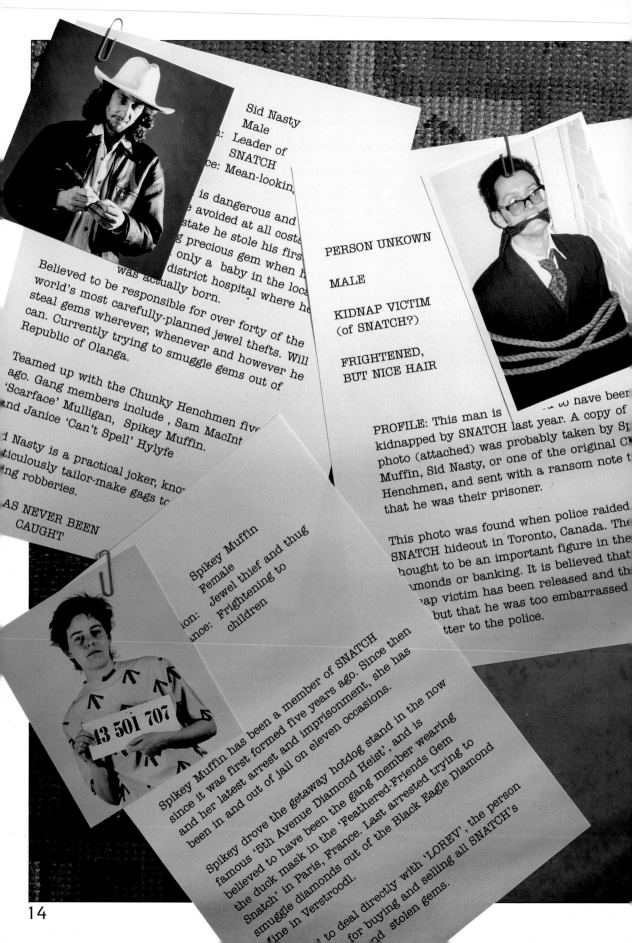

Sid Nasty
Male
...n: Leader of
SNATCH
...ce: Mean-lookin...

...is dangerous and ...
...e avoided at all cost...
...state he stole his firs...
...g precious gem when h...
...only a baby in the loca...
...district hospital where he...
was actually born.

Believed to be responsible for over forty of the
world's most carefully-planned jewel thefts. Will
steal gems wherever, whenever and however he
can. Currently trying to smuggle gems out of
Republic of Olanga.

Teamed up with the Chunky Henchmen five ...
ago. Gang members include , Sam MacInt...
'Scarface' Mulligan, Spikey Muffin, ...
and Janice 'Can't Spell' Hylyfe

...d Nasty is a practical joker, kno...
...ticulously tailor-make gags to ...
...ing robberies.

...AS NEVER BEEN
CAUGHT

PERSON UNKOWN

MALE

KIDNAP VICTIM
(of SNATCH?)

FRIGHTENED,
BUT NICE HAIR

PROFILE: This man is ... ...o have been
kidnapped by SNATCH last year. A copy of ...
photo (attached) was probably taken by Sp...
Muffin, Sid Nasty, or one of the original C...
Henchmen, and sent with a ransom note t...
that he was their prisoner.

This photo was found when police raided ...
SNATCH hideout in Toronto, Canada. The...
...hought to be an important figure in the...
...amonds or banking. It is believed that ...
...nap victim has been released and th...
...but that he was too embarrassed ...
...tter to the police.

Spikey Muffin
Female
Jewel thief and thug
...ion: Frightening to
children

Spikey Muffin has been a member of SNATCH
since it was first formed five years ago. Since then
and her latest arrest and imprisonment, she has
been in and out of jail on eleven occasions.

Spikey drove the getaway hotdog stand in the now
famous '5th Avenue Diamond Heist', and is
believed to have been the gang member wearing
the duck mask in the 'Feathered-Friends Gem
Snatch' in Paris, France. Last arrested trying to
smuggle diamonds out of the Black Eagle Diamond
fine in Verstroodl.

...to deal directly with 'LOREV', the person
... for buying and selling all SNATCH's
...d stolen gems.

14

Ed Meanstreets
Male
ation: Private Investigator
& Dry Cleaner
pearance: Great from the
front

reets owns a successful dry cleaning
with branches throughout Europe and
the U.S., offering special rates for detective
busi
raincoats.

He has also devoted his life to trying t
down anyone trying to steal diamonds
Black Eagle Diamond Mining Corporation

Meanstreets has successfully captured twen
four members of SNATCH on fifteen separate
occasions.

MISSING . . . POSSIBLY KIDNAPPED . . .
POSSIBLY NOW WORKING FOR SNATCH . . .

A GALLERY OF ROGUES

Time: Monday, 5:25pm
Place: The floor of the office of Mrs. Gertrude Rook

With no one around, you take the opportunity to catch
up on some reading. You start by going through the file
of papers that caught your eye. You spread everything
out on the floor – it's the only clear space you can find.

*What do you think the letters SNATCH might
stand for?*

GLITTERING PRIZES

Time: Wednesday, 10:30am
Place: Workshop, 1st Floor,
Hans Anderfeet Diamond Merchants

It's time to speak to Christen Hans Anderfeet, down on the list as a 'diamond expert'. Sitting at his workbench, he claims to know nothing about the *Black Diamond* in particular or Olangan jewels in general. "I never use any stones from the Republic of Olanga," he says.

Do you believe him?

SPILLING THE BEANS

Time: Wednesday, 1:15pm
Place: Foyer, *Hotel New Amsterdam*

You've been followed by a woman since you left the diamond merchant and now she's shadowed you back to your hotel. You bump into her to see if she panics. Instead, she drops her bag and everything spills out. Nothing much here, but that key-ring looks rather interesting, and what about that photo? The dreadful rhyme is certainly good news.

Why and how?

Fellow henchmen
and henchwomen:

If you take my eye
to be your bee
The rest is simple,
you'll agree.

It will make my jay
your sea
And later make
my bee be you.

Don't believe me?
Try. It's true.

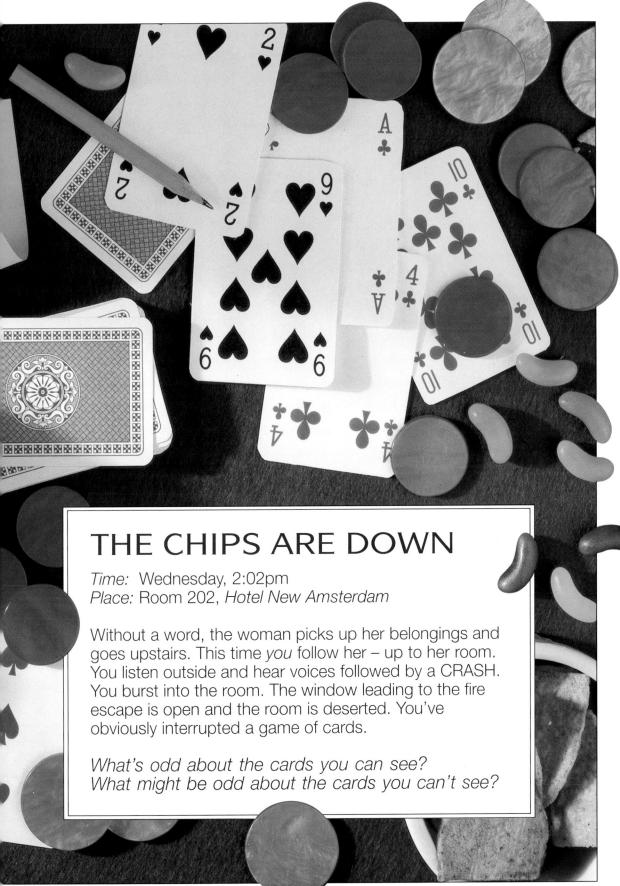

THE CHIPS ARE DOWN

Time: Wednesday, 2:02pm
Place: Room 202, *Hotel New Amsterdam*

Without a word, the woman picks up her belongings and
goes upstairs. This time *you* follow her – up to her room.
You listen outside and hear voices followed by a CRASH.
You burst into the room. The window leading to the fire
escape is open and the room is deserted. You've
obviously interrupted a game of cards.

What's odd about the cards you can see?
What might be odd about the cards you can't see?

ROOM SERVICE

Time: Wednesday, 2:34pm
Place: Room 234, *Hotel New Amsterdam*

You go back to your own room to find that the place has been searched from top to bottom. Even your toothpaste tube has been emptied. A far from friendly message is stuck to your pillow with a hatpin. But that's not all that your unwelcome intruder has left behind.

What telltale clues suggest the identity of the unwelcome visitor?

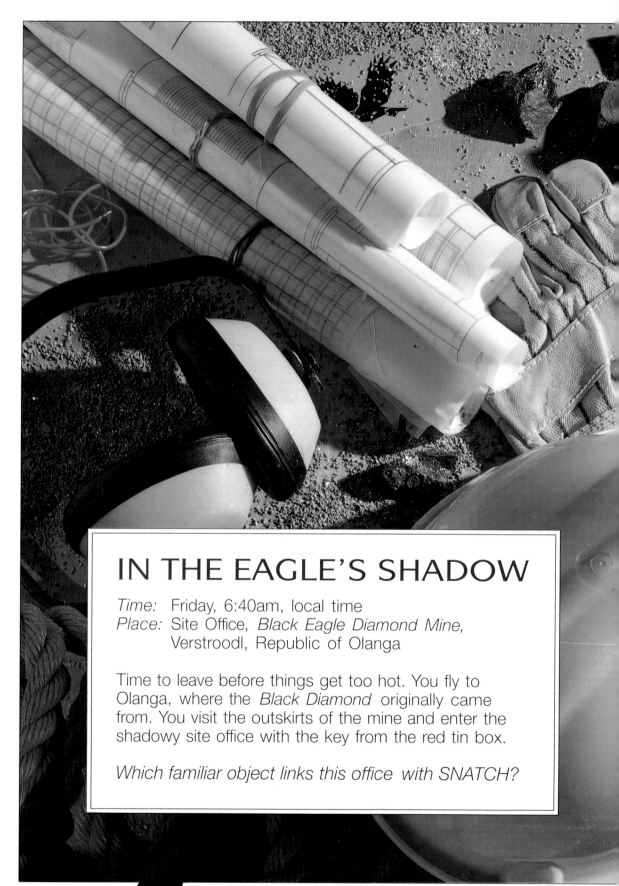

IN THE EAGLE'S SHADOW

Time: Friday, 6:40am, local time
Place: Site Office, *Black Eagle Diamond Mine,*
Verstroodl, Republic of Olanga

Time to leave before things get too hot. You fly to Olanga, where the *Black Diamond* originally came from. You visit the outskirts of the mine and enter the shadowy site office with the key from the red tin box.

Which familiar object links this office with SNATCH?

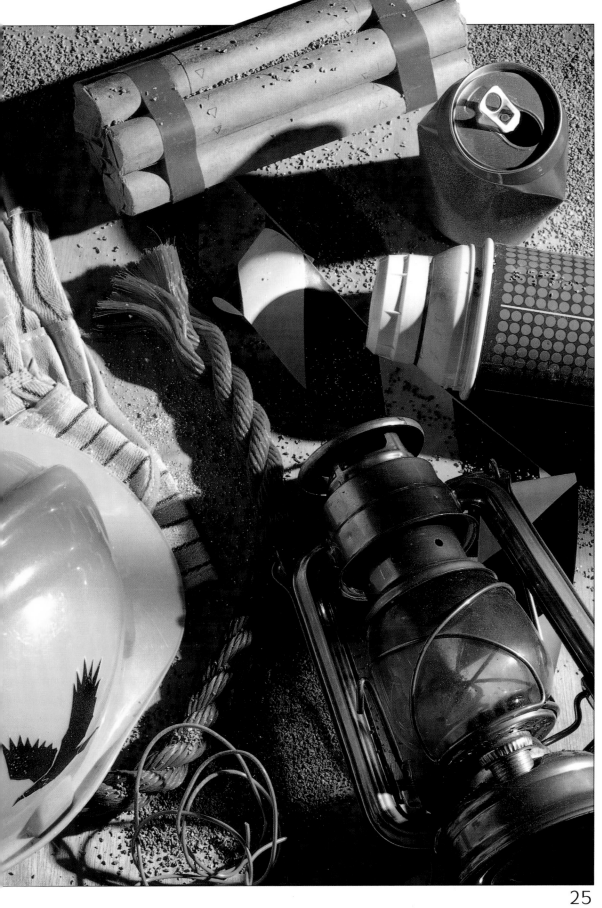

UNDER ARREST

Time: Friday, 8:11am
Place: Captain Appul's Office,
Verstroodl Police Headquarters, Olanga

Caught snooping by the local cops, you've been taken in for questioning. The phone rings and the captain leaves you alone for a moment. You may be handcuffed, but you can still use your eyes. The drawer in his desk is open, so who can blame you for taking a peep?

What vital piece of information lurks among the mess?

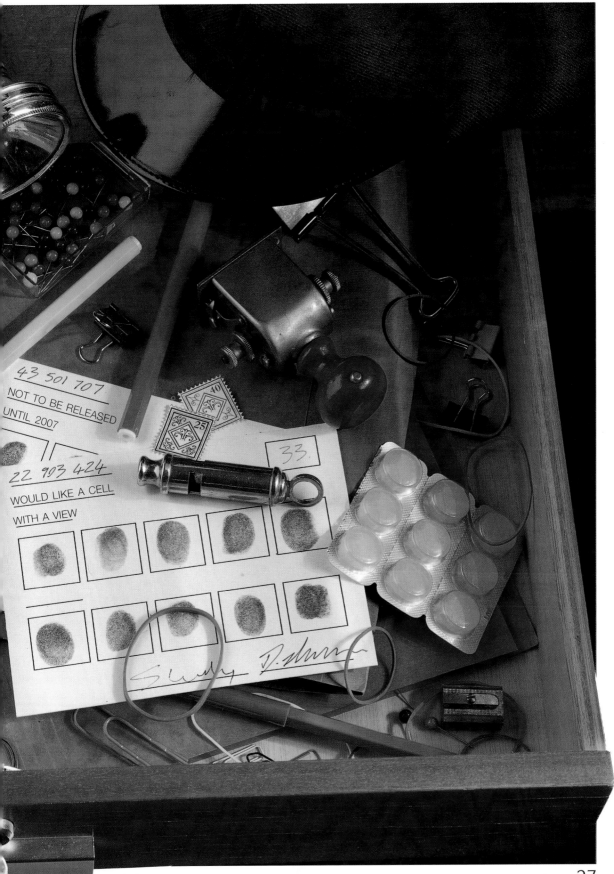

43 501 707

NOT TO BE RELEASED
UNTIL 2007

22 903 424

WOULD LIKE A CELL

WITH A VIEW

33.

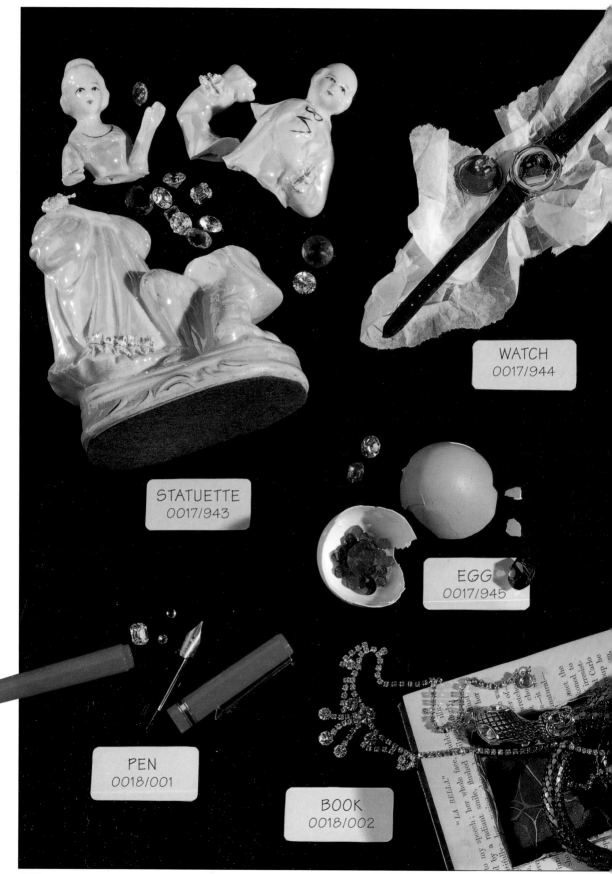

WATCH
0017/944

STATUETTE
0017/943

EGG
0017/945

PEN
0018/001

BOOK
0018/002

SMUGGLERS' HOARDS

Time: Friday, 11:29am, local time
Place: Evidence & Confiscation Vault,
     Verstroodl Police Headquarters, Olanga

Having convinced Captain Appul that you're one of the
good guys, you are taken downstairs – not to a cell, but
to this windowless, dusty vault. Here, the captain
shows you a display of some of the items used by
crooks trying to smuggle gems out of the country.

Which item is of particular interest?

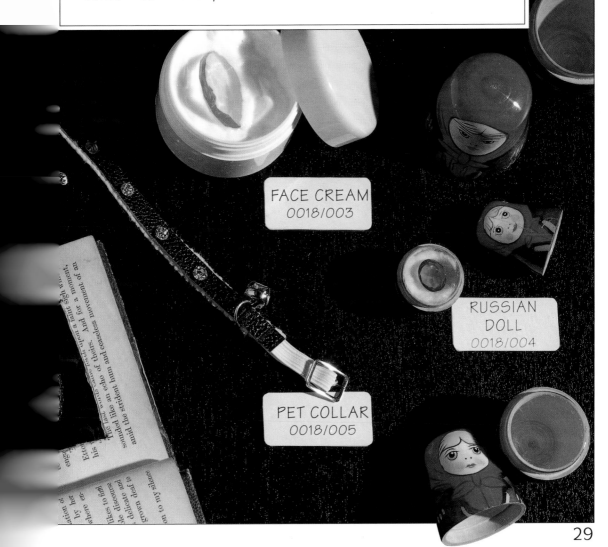

FACE CREAM
0018/003

RUSSIAN
DOLL
0018/004

PET COLLAR
0018/005

It is the most widely burned fossil fuel in Olanga.

That is why this carbon-based fuel (not shown here) is sometimes referred to as black diamond.

NOTE: Rocks shown here relate to text on page 23.

- 24 -

[See page 156.]

ALL STAFF ARE INVITED TO PROFESSOR POFFLE'S "BRING-A-ROCK PARTY" THIS FRIDAY.

MINERAL WATER WILL BE PROVIDED

BANG
...ian eruptions occur wh...
...extremely viscous.
...d gases cause massive
...sions to occur as they
...ape. During the explosions,
...ge amounts of volcanic ash are
...hrown high into the air.

One type of movement at plate boundaries involves one plate plunging below another. Some scientists think this sets off all the other movements. At some boundaries, molten rock rises between two plates.

This hardens onto the plate edges, pushing the plates apart. this may set off all other plate movement.
[See page 156.]

The Big Yawn Coal Mine
Fact Sheet 11
Diamond is made from carbon and coal is too – but its carbon atoms are arranged differently. That is why one is a sparkling gem and the other is the most commonly used fossil fuel in Olanga.
Wheelhouse

The manager of the staff canteen has instructed that no further meals will be served until scientists stop hiding minerals in the rock cake.

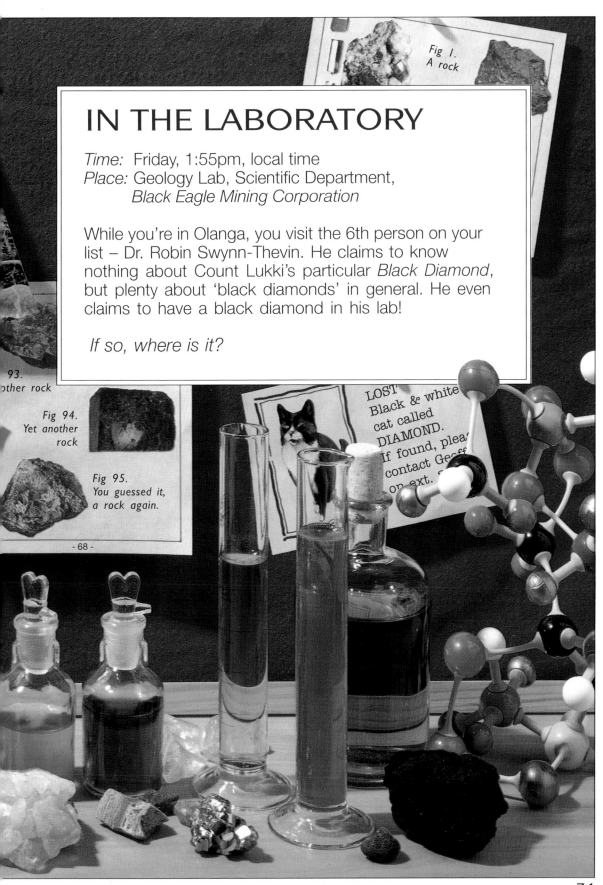

IN THE LABORATORY

Time: Friday, 1:55pm, local time
Place: Geology Lab, Scientific Department,
Black Eagle Mining Corporation

While you're in Olanga, you visit the 6th person on your list – Dr. Robin Swynn-Thevin. He claims to know nothing about Count Lukki's particular *Black Diamond*, but plenty about 'black diamonds' in general. He even claims to have a black diamond in his lab!

If so, where is it?

Fig 1.
A rock

93.
other rock

Fig 94.
Yet another
rock

Fig 95.
You guessed it,
a rock again.

- 68 -

LOST
Black & white
cat called
DIAMOND.
If found, plea
contact Ge
on ext.

HATS OFF TO PERCY

Time: Monday, 10:00am precisely
Place: The manager's outer office,
   Snoots & Co Bank, London, England

Now it's off to London. You're waiting to be shown into the manager's inner office. It was he who originally arranged to ship the *Black Diamond* from Olanga to Count Lukki back in 1990. There's not much to look at apart from the hats and scarfs hanging on the wall . . . but there's something here that's naggingly familiar.

What is it?

OTS & CO BANK

Smart
Manager

43718

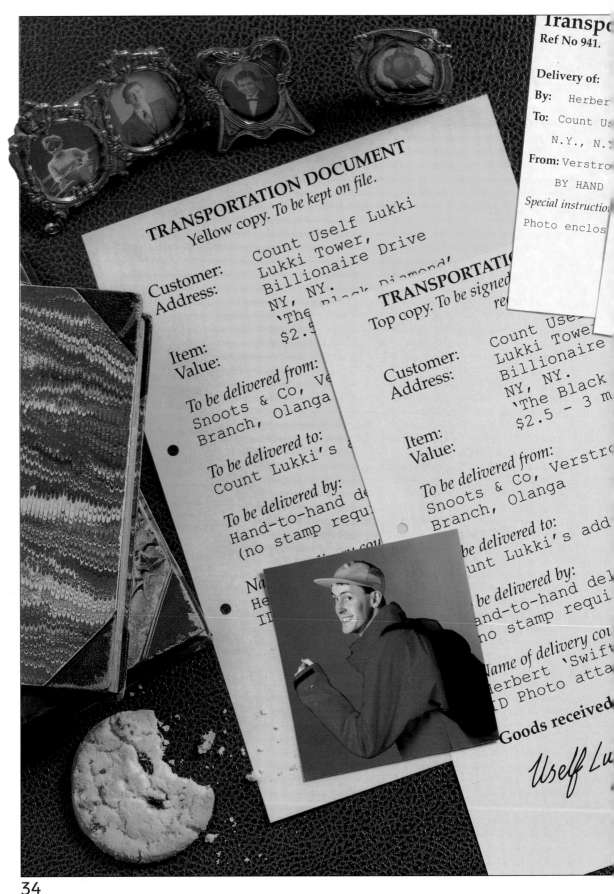

Delivery of:

By: Herber

To: Count Us

      N.Y., N.Y

From: Verstro

      BY HAND

Special instructio

Photo enclos

TRANSPORTATION DOCUMENT
Yellow copy. To be kept on file.

Customer: Count Uself Lukki
            Lukki Tower,
Address: Billionaire Drive
            NY, NY.
            'The Black Diamond'
            $2.5

Item:
Value:

To be delivered from:
Snoots & Co, Ve
Branch, Olanga

To be delivered to:
Count Lukki's a

To be delivered by:
Hand-to-hand de
(no stamp requi

Na
He
II

TRANSPORTATIO
Top copy. To be signed
re

Customer: Count Use
            Lukki Towe
Address: Billionaire
            NY, NY.
            'The Black
            $2.5 - 3 m

Item:
Value:

To be delivered from:
Snoots & Co, Verstro
Branch, Olanga

be delivered to:
unt Lukki's add

be delivered by:
and-to-hand del
no stamp requi

Name of delivery cou
Herbert 'Swift
ID Photo atta

Goods received

Uself Lu

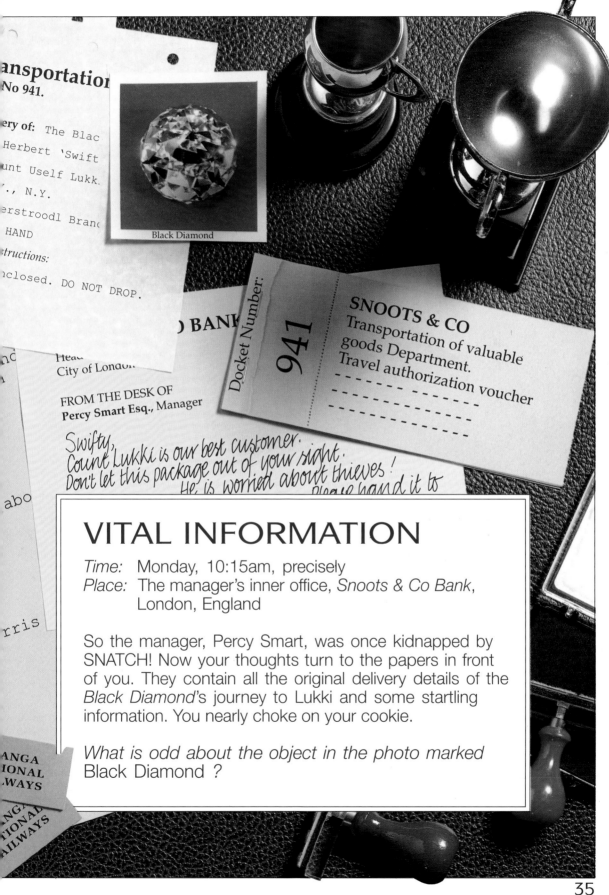

ansportatio
No 941.

ery of: The Blac
Herbert 'Swift
unt Uself Lukk.
., N.Y.
erstroodl Bran
HAND
tructions:
closed. DO NOT DROP.

Black Diamond

D BANK

Hea
City of Londo

FROM THE DESK OF
Percy Smart Esq., Manager

Docket Number:

941

SNOOTS & CO
Transportation of valuable
goods Department.
Travel authorization voucher
- - - - - - - - - - - - - - - -
- - - - - - - - - - - - - -
- - - - - - - - - - - -

Swifty,
Count Lukki is our best customer.
Don't let this package out of your sight.
He is worried about thieves!
please hand it to

abo

rris

ANGA
IONAL
WAYS

NGA
IONAL
ILWAYS

VITAL INFORMATION

Time: Monday, 10:15am, precisely
Place: The manager's inner office, *Snoots & Co Bank*,
London, England

So the manager, Percy Smart, was once kidnapped by
SNATCH! Now your thoughts turn to the papers in front
of you. They contain all the original delivery details of the
Black Diamond's journey to Lukki and some startling
information. You nearly choke on your cookie.

What is odd about the object in the photo marked
Black Diamond ?

36

GERTRUDE AND ARCHIE'S

Time: Wednesday, 4:25pm
Place: 42, Raymond Chandler Drive,
Home of Gertrude and Archie Rook

Time to try to talk to Lukki's lawyer again, or even to her husband, Archie. This time you try them at home. On the front door is the note: *Hello. Door open. Please leave groceries on kitchen table.* You go inside. There's another note. This one is pinned to the wall the wrong way around, but with the words showing through the paper.

Where should you find Archie?

QUALITY JEWELS
AT GIVEAWAY PRICES

Great sale
today.
Everything
must go!

JAKE'S JEWELS & GEMS

SMASH 'N' GRAB

Time: Wednesday, 4:50pm
Place: Outside *Jake's Jewels 'n' Gems*

Archie Rook's message brings you to the right place, but a little late. You're greeted by a broken window. Archie's 'appointment' was a smash and grab raid! There aren't many jewels remaining, but something far more significant has been left at the scene of the crime.

Who does it belong to?

FOOD FOR THOUGHT

Time: Wednesday, 8:00pm
Place: The late Count Uself Lukki's apartment,
New York, New York

You end your mission at the home of 'Mr. Diamond'
himself. You have a typed list of the suspects in front of
you, surrounded by one collection the Count didn't
leave to any institute – a rare selection of silk fruit and
vegetables. You should now have enough information
to answer this key question before turning to page 48:

Who stole the Black Diamond?

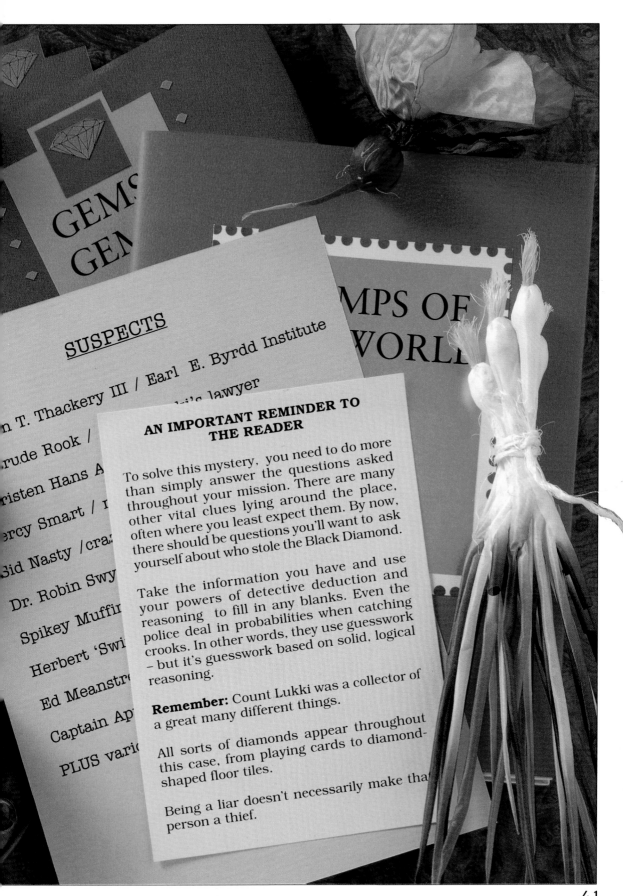

GEMS
GEM

MPS OF
VORLE

SUSPECTS

n T. Thackery III / Earl E. Byrdd Institute

rude Rook /

risten Hans A

ci's lawyer

rcy Smart / r

id Nasty /cra

Dr. Robin Swy

Spikey Muffir

Herbert 'Swi

Ed Meanstre

Captain Ap

PLUS varic

AN IMPORTANT REMINDER TO THE READER

To solve this mystery, you need to do more than simply answer the questions asked throughout your mission. There are many other vital clues lying around the place, often where you least expect them. By now, there should be questions you'll want to ask yourself about who stole the Black Diamond.

Take the information you have and use your powers of detective deduction and reasoning to fill in any blanks. Even the police deal in probabilities when catching crooks. In other words, they use guesswork – but it's guesswork based on solid, logical reasoning.

Remember: Count Lukki was a collector of a great many different things.

All sorts of diamonds appear throughout this case, from playing cards to diamond-shaped floor tiles.

Being a liar doesn't necessarily make tha person a thief.

HELPFUL HINTS

Pages 2 & 3
The answers are there in black and white. Read everything carefully.

Pages 4 & 5
The labels are in the Earl E. Byrdd Institute's catalogue code. This uses a reverse alphabet running from Z-A.

Pages 6 & 7
Don't forget the framed photos.

Pages 8 & 9
Turn the parcel the right way up and try tackling the bottom right hand corner first.

Pages 10 & 11
The bird looks like an eagle. Wasn't there something about an eagle in one of the newspaper clippings?

Pages 12 & 13
Check the symbols on the files carefully.

Pages 14 & 15
Sid Nasty's initials are S.N. and the 'A' of SNATCH could be for 'And'... but 'Sid Nasty And' whom? The answer is in the documents somewhere.

Pages 16 & 17
Look again. The answer lies in the uncut diamonds.

Pages 18 & 19
Read out loud, some of the words sound like letters. Could this be the key to an earlier message?

Pages 20 & 21
Compare these cards with the ones on Thackery's desk (pages 6 & 7).

Pages 22 & 23
The intruder is bad at spelling. Hmmm. He, or she, has also dropped something you've seen before.

Pages 24 & 25
The answer lies on the card table back at the *Hotel New Amsterdam*.

Pages 26 & 27
Check the prisoner numbers on the fingerprint cards against any other prisoner numbers you might have seen.

Pages 28 & 29
You've seen one of them before.

Pages 30 & 31
The answer is somewhere in those notices.

Pages 32 & 33
You've seen him in another photograph, but he didn't look so happy then.

Pages 34 & 35
You've already seen two objects that look very like it. Can you remember where?

Pages 36 & 37
Read the note Archie has pinned to the wall the wrong way around. You'll get it in time.

Pages 38 & 39
That nail picker looks familiar.

Pages 40 & 41
These are Count Lukki's books. Anything to do with his collections?

ANSWERS

Pages 2 & 3
The answer to both these questions can be found
on page 3, in the newspaper article entitled **'Safe and
well'**. The *Black Diamond* is worth $2.5m. The
missing safe was found under Archie Rook's bed.

Pages 4 & 5
Count Lukki's name has two Ks in it. The only label with two identical letters next
to each other is the one attached to the stamp album. It reads 'Ofppr', so,
presumably, O=L, F=U, P=K and R=I.
The labels were encoded at the Institute by writing out the alphabet, then,
underneath, writing the alphabet in reverse, like this:

A B C D E F G H I J K L M N O P Q R S T U V W X Y Z
Z Y X W V U T S R Q P O N M L K J I H G F E D C B A

Each letter in the top row stands for the letter directly below it. Using
this code, 'LUKKI' matches up with 'OFPPR'. The count therefore must
have donated the stamp album. Using the same key to decode the
other labels, you'll find that the medals were
donated by someone called HAROLD SMITH,
the butterflies by WILSON, the coins by JIM
CARTER and the plants by MARY RICKS.

Pages 6 & 7
There is the large gem-like paperweight on the desk by the photograph of
Gideon T. Thackery III and his wife. She is wearing jewels. The cat in the other
photograph also appears to be wearing jewels – a diamond-studded collar.

Pages 8 & 9
The writing is in English, but with the letters divided into groups of five instead of
words, and the message starting in the bottom right hand corner instead of the top
left. With punctuation, the advice reads: **NOT TO BE OPENED WITH ANYONE
ELSE AROUND. O.K.?**

Pages 10 & 11
The black bird on the green swipe card is an eagle. The eight
stones on the box are uncut diamonds. The map appears to
be of a mine. There was a *Black Eagle Diamond Mine*
mentioned in one of the newspaper clippings on
pages 2 & 3.

Pages 12 & 13
Yes. This file has the same symbol on it as the 'swipe card'.

Pages 14 & 15
SNATCH, the international jewel thief gang, stands for **Si**d **N**asty **A**nd **T**he **C**hunky **H**enchmen. In Nasty's profile, it mentions that he joined up with the Chunky Henchmen five years ago.

Pages 16 & 17
The black zip bag full of uncut diamonds obviously comes from the *Black Eagle Diamond Mine*. You can see part of the eagle symbol showing through. You know that the mine is in Verstroodl from the report on Spikey Muffin in Gertrude Rook's office on pages 14 & 15. You know from the newspaper clippings on pages 2 & 3 that Verstroodl is in Olanga. These stones must come from Olanga. Therefore Christen Hans Anderfeet must be lying.

Pages 18 & 19
This poem is the key to a code. It tells us which letters to substitute for which. **'If you take my eye to be your bee'** means that, when decoding a message, the letter 'i' becomes 'b'. It goes on to say that **'It will make my jay your sea'**. This means that the letter 'j' will be decoded as a 'c'. **'And later make my bee be you'** means that the letter 'b' should be decoded as a letter 'u'.

To find out all the other letters of the code, you have to find a sequence which fits in with the letters you already know. The top row represents the letters in the message, and the bottom row the letters which they stand for.

A B C D E F G H I J K L M N O P Q R S T U V W X Y Z
T U V W X Y Z A B C D E F G H I J K L M N O P Q R S

With this, you can now decode the message from the red tin box which the woman gave you gift-wrapped at the cafe on pages 8 & 9.

The decoded message reads: **The Key Opens the Site Office to the B.E.D.M. What You Need is in there. SNATCH.**
'B.E.D.M.' must stand for the *Black Eagle Diamond Mine*.

Pages 20 & 21

Cards come in four suits: clubs, spades, hearts and diamonds. With cards from an ordinary pack – such as those on Gideon T. Thackery III's desk on pages 6 & 7 – clubs and spades are black, and hearts and diamonds are red. What's odd about the cards we can see on this table is that the clubs and spades are red, and the hearts are black. This suggests that the missing cards have *black diamonds* on them.

Pages 22 & 23

There is a diamond ring lying in the folds of the bedclothes. You've seen the ring on the finger of the woman who slipped you the package on pages 8 & 9. Then there is the spelling in the note. It's very bad.

The card players who dashed away from Room 202 are most likely to be members of SNATCH. The weird playing cards tie in with Sid Nasty's practical jokes and sense of fun. The initials S.N. on the scorepad are most likely his. According to information in one of the reports in Gertrude Rook's office (on pages 14 & 15) another member of SNATCH is named 'Janice 'Can't Spell' Hylyfe'. So perhaps Janice Hylyfe, the woman who has been following you, the woman who gave you the package, and the woman who left the badly-spelled note are all one and the same.

Pages 24 & 25

There was a similar red and silver can lying on the card table in Room 202 of the *Hotel New Amsterdam* on pages 20 & 21.

Pages 26 & 27

The bottom fingerprint card has the numbers '43 501 707' on it. These match the prison number held up by Spikey Muffin in her photograph on pages 14 & 15. Written on the fingerprint card are the words 'NOT TO BE RELEASED UNTIL THE YEAR 2007', which means that Spikey Muffin must still be in jail from when the photo was taken . . . and will be for a long time. Because the files in Gertrude Rook's office were so dusty, they must have been lying there for quite a while, and so must the photo . . . this suggests that Spikey Muffin has already been behind bars for some time. This means that the initials 'S.M.' on the pad on the card table (pages 20 & 21) don't belong to her, but to Sam MacIntosh – another gang member referred to in the files on pages 14 & 15.

Pages 28 & 29

The diamond-studded pet collar looks familiar. On Gideon T. Thackery III's desk, back at the Earl E. Byrdd Institute, there is a framed photograph of his cat wearing a similar collar. Could it be the *same* collar?

Pages 30 & 31

Yes, one of the pages on the board reads '... that is why this carbon-based fuel . . . is sometimes referred to as 'black diamond'. It is the most widely burned fossil fuel in Olanga'. Fact sheet 11 on 'The Big Yawn' Coal Mine mentions that 'Diamond is made from carbon and coal is too – but its carbon atoms are arranged differently.' It goes on to refer to coal as 'the most commonly used fossil fuel in Olanga'. The fuel referred to in the first notice must, therefore, be coal. So coal is sometimes called 'Black Diamond', and there is a lump of coal on the lab top! A dead end here.

Pages 32 & 33

The last time you saw Mr. Percy Smart, manager of *Snoots & Co Bank*, he was in this photograph in the file at Gertrude Rook's office on pages 14 & 15. He was bound and gagged and described as being an unidentified kidnap victim of SNATCH. Perhaps they forced him to work for them? It's not the sort of question you can ask him really . . .

Pages 34 & 35

The so-called 'Black Diamond' in the photograph looks just like the crystal paperweight on the desk in the acting assistant deputy curator's office on pages 6 & 7. There is a similar paperweight – though covered in dust – in Gertrude Rook's office on pages 12 & 13. Surely this can't really be the real *Black Diamond*? In one of the newspaper clippings on pages 2 & 3, it is stated that 'Though extremely rich, Count Lukki was in the habit of giving his friends the same gift every year: a cut-glass paperweight.'

Pages 36 & 37

Archie Rook has left his wife Gertrude a list of what he plans to do today, but pinned it to the wall the wrong way around. You can, however, still see the writing through the paper. If you look at the time (4:25pm) and read the back-to-front letters, you'll see the entry: *'Some time between 4 o'clock and 5 o'clock, I plan to do some window shopping at Jake's Jewels 'n' Gems.'* That's where he should be. It's a shop about twenty-five minutes from the Rooks' house.

Did you also spot that the cut-in-half red and silver can containing gems is just like the one on the SNATCH members' card table in Room 202 of the Hotel New Amsterdam (on pages 20 & 21), and like the crushed can in the site office at the Black Eagle Diamond Mine on pages 24 & 25. Archie Rook must be involved in diamond smuggling with SNATCH!

Pages 38 & 39

Sid Nasty, leader of SNATCH. The object is the black dagger, studded with gems, sticking out from under a tray of rings. You've seen it before in black and white. In the photo of Nasty in the file on pages 14 & 15, he's cleaning his nails with it. Nasty may be the mastermind behind the world's most successful jewel thefts but - as his profile says - he **'will steal gems wherever and whenever possible'**.

Pages 40 & 41

So you want to know who stole the *Black Diamond*? Well, you won't find the answer on this page. This is your one last chance to make up your mind who *you* think did it. Remember all those points in **"An important reminder to the reader"**. Ready? Then turn the page and hold it up against a mirror . . .

THE SOLUTION

Count Lukki is described as a 'philatelist', as well as a gem collector in a newspaper clipping on page 2. As the dictionary definition on page 3 explains, a philatelist is someone who collects stamps.

In the paperwork in the manager's office at Snoots & Co Bank, on pages 34 & 35, you learn that the package said to include the Black Diamond was sent by courier. The package was put in the hands of Herbert 'Swifty' Morris who, in turn, went from Olanga to New York to hand it directly to Count Lukki in person. Why, then, was there a stamp on the box when – in the paperwork on pages 34 & 35 – it clearly states 'hand-to-hand delivery', no stamp required.?

In Count Lukki's instructions in his will, quoted by Gertrude Sparrow in a newspaper clipping on page 3, it states that Thackery was to be sent the Black Diamond 'along with the original packaging with which he, the Count, first received it from Olanga'. It goes on to say that 'Thackery was an expert and that he would realize the Black Diamond's great value,' when he saw it. Notice Lukki was careful to avoid saying that he received the Black Diamond in the package . . . which could suggest that it was never in it, but if not in it, where? On it, perhaps?

A number of stamps have appeared throughout the mission. Some of those in the album donated to the Earl E. Byrdd Institute by Lukki, on pages 4 & 5, have a similar diamond-shaped design in the middle to those in Captain Appul's drawer at Verstrootl Police H.Q. on pages 26 & 27. They are, in fact, Olangan stamps . . . But there was only one black Olangan stamp with the diamond motif, and that was stuck to the original package. You can see it in the acting assistant deputy curator's office on pages 6 & 7.

In fact, the Olangan Black Diamond is not a precious gem at all. It is one of the rarest stamps in history – known only to a handful of the most expert of expert stamp collectors. No wonder everyone, including Sid Nasty and SNATCH thought it must be a real diamond! Count Lukki was always worried about thieves, so decided to use a trick. He arranged for a worthless paperweight to be put inside the package, and the $2.5m Black Diamond stamp to be stuck on the outside. A thief would never realize that the stamp itself was the prize!

But Lukki knew that Thackery would know what it was and how valuable it was – he said as much in a newspaper article. But, when Lukki died and the institute inherited the package, Thackery claimed that the Black Diamond was missing. In fact, he even went along with pretending that he thought it was a real diamond. That was because Thackery planned to remove the Black Diamond from the package, once the fuss had died down. His wife has expensive tastes for jewels and he'd arranged to sell the stamp in secret to buy more for her.

If that's not proof enough, think back to Thackery's office when he was called away to speak to someone named Olive. If you use the same code as used by the institute to denote who donated what, you'll find OLIVE comes out as LOREV. This is the name of the top dealer in stolen goods mentioned in Gertrude Rook's file on Spikey Muffin.

It was Thackery who stole the Black Diamond. Did you catch him?